THE **CAT** THAT DISAPPEARED

MY FIRST GRAPHIC NOVELS ARE PUBLISHED BY STONE ARCH BOOKS
A CAPSTONE IMPRINT
1710 ROE CREST DRIVE
NORTH MANKATO, MINNESOTA 56003
WWW.CAPSTONEPUB.COM

Library of Congress Cataloging-in-Publication data is available on the Library of Congress website.

Library Binding: 978-1-4342-1887-2
Paperback: 978-1-4342-2282-4

Summary: Ava's cat goes missing right before the pet show. Ava, Clair, and Caleb have to find Oatmeal before the show begins.

Art Director: BOB LENTZ
Graphic Designer: EMILY HARRIS
Production Specialist: MICHELLE BIEDSCHEID

Printed in the United States     4161

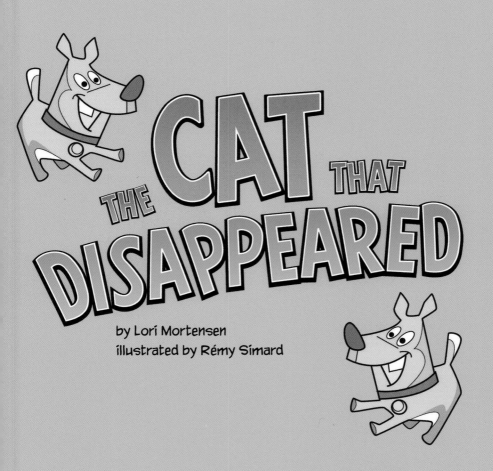

# THE CAT THAT DISAPPEARED

by Lori Mortensen

illustrated by Rémy Simard

STONE ARCH BOOKS
a capstone imprint

# HOW TO READ A GRAPHIC NOVEL

Graphic novels are easy to read. Boxes called panels show you how to follow the story. Look at the panels from left to right and top to bottom.

Read the word boxes and word balloons from left to right as well. Don't forget the sound and action words in the pictures.

The pictures and the words work together to tell the whole story.

Ava was bored. So was her cat, Oatmeal.

Then Ava had an idea.

She grabbed her phone and called her friends.

Clair brought her dog. Caleb brought his snake.

They made a stage in Ava's backyard. They also made signs.

They set up chairs.

But by showtime, Oatmeal had disappeared.

Ava and her friends searched outside.
Ava looked in the big tree.

Clair looked in the garden.

Caleb looked under the car.

No one could find Oatmeal.

Ava and her friends searched inside. Ava
looked under the sofa.

Clair looked under the bed.

Caleb looked in the closet.

They still couldn't find Oatmeal.

Ava had a new idea.

Instead of having a pet show, they would become detectives.

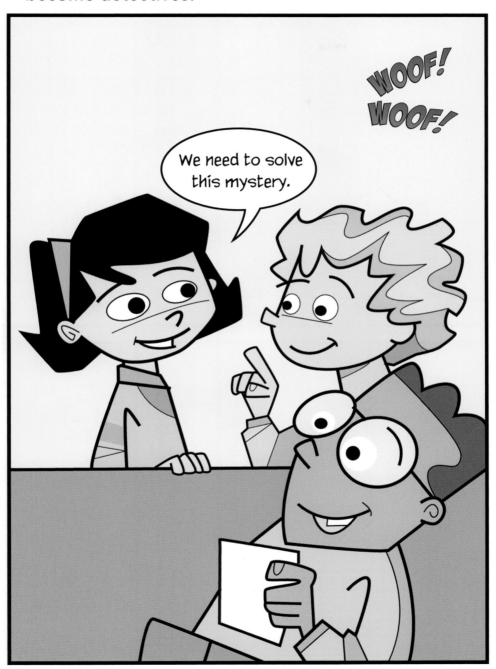

Ava and her friends went back outside. They looked for clues.

They searched under all the chairs, but
Oatmeal wasn't there.

Suddenly, Ava heard a familiar noise.

They ran across the yard, but it wasn't Oatmeal.

It was the neighbor's cat.

The neighbor's cat ran away.

But Clair's dog kept barking. Ava wished he
would stop.

# Who could think about clues with all that noise?

Then Ava stopped covering her ears. She'd been ignoring the biggest and loudest clue of all!

Ava raced to the shed and opened the door.

Ava's pet show was a hit. Caleb's snake won a prize for the longest pet.

Clair's dog won for the loudest pet.

And Oatmeal won a prize for his disappearing act.

# GLOSSARY

**CLUES** (KLOOZ) — things that help you find the answer to a mystery

**DETECTIVES** (di-TEK-tivz) — people who try to solve mysteries or crimes

**DISAPPEARED** (diss-up-PIHRD) — to go missing

**FAMILIAR** (fuh-MIL-yur) — something a person knows very well

**IGNORING** (ig-NOR-ing) — not paying attention to something

**MYSTERY** (MISS-tur-ee) — something that is hard to understand or explain

**SEARCHED** (SURCHD) — looked for something

# DISCUSSION QUESTIONS

**1.** Do you have any pets? If so, what are they? If not, do you want a pet?

**2.** Ava decides she wants to have a pet show. Have you ever been part of a show? If so, what was it?

**3.** Do you want to be a detective? Why or why not?

# WRITING PROMPTS

**1.** To find Oatmeal, Ava and her friends become detectives. Make a list of supplies you would need if you were a detective.

**2.** At the end of the story, each animal wins a prize. Make a new prize for each animal. Write down the new prizes and the reasons why each animal got the prize listed.

**3.** Did you know where Oatmeal was? Look through the book and write down clues you find.

# MY 1ST GRAPHIC NOVEL®

# THE 1ST STEP INTO GRAPHIC NOVELS

These books are the perfect introduction to the world of safe, appealing graphic novels. Each story uses familiar topics, repeating patterns, and core vocabulary words appropriate for a beginning reader. Combine the entertaining story with comic book panels, exciting action elements, and bright colors and a safe graphic novel is born.